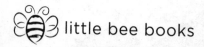 little bee books

An imprint of Bonnier Publishing USA
251 Park Avenue South, New York, NY 10010
Copyright © 2018 by Bonnier Publishing USA
All rights reserved, including the right of
reproduction in whole or in part in any form.
Little Bee Books is a registered trademark of Bonnier Publishing USA,
and associated colophon is a trademark of Bonnier Publishing USA.
Printed in China TPL 0318
ISBN: 978-1-4998-0605-2 (hc)
First Edition 10 9 8 7 6 5 4 3 2 1
ISBN: 978-1-4998-0604-5 (pbk)
First Edition 10 9 8 7 6 5 4 3 2 1

Library of Congress Cataloging-in-Publication Data
is available upon request.

littlebeebooks.com
bonnierpublishingusa.com

Tales of
SASHA

Showtime!

by Alexa Pearl
illustrated by Paco Sordo

little bee books

Contents

Dance Party

"Let's dance!" called Sasha.

Sasha swished her tail. She tapped her hooves. She trotted in a circle with her sisters, Zara and Poppy.

"Make room for me," Kimani said, dancing into their circle. She high-stepped and pranced.

"Go, Kimani! Go, Kimani!" chanted Sasha. Her sisters joined in.

Kimani twirled. Her purple wings fluttered. She rose above the grass.

"Whoa! Keep those hooves on the ground," Sasha warned her friend.

"Oops! I forgot I was in Verdant Valley," said Kimani.

Kimani was a flying horse. She lived in Crystal Cove with other flying horses. The horses in Verdant Valley didn't fly. None of them had wings, except for Sasha. She'd only just found out that she was a flying horse, too!

Twinkle danced over to the group. She strutted into the middle of the circle and twirled. Sasha cheered. Her friend from Verdant Valley was a great dancer!

"Coming in!" Wyatt clopped into the circle. He tried to lift his hooves. "Whoops!" He knocked into Zara. "Pardon me!" He then knocked into Poppy.

Wyatt backed out of the circle, his head low. "I'm too clumsy to dance."

"No, you're not." Sasha gave her best friend an encouraging nuzzle. "And even if you are, it doesn't matter. It's a welcome-home celebration for all of us."

Wyatt and Sasha had just come home from the Royal Island. Sasha had met her birth parents, the King and Queen of the flying horses, for the first time.

Sasha waved her adoptive mother and father over to join the circle.

"I twisted my ankle in the field. I can't dance today," her mom said.

"Count me out, too," added her dad.

"Big surprise," joked Sasha. Her dad didn't dance . . . ever.

Suddenly, a glossy black bird soared down from the clouds.

"It's the toucan!" cried Kimani.

The toucan had come from Crystal Cove. He was the special messenger for the flying horses. He landed gently on Kimani's back.

"Greetings! I have a message for Sasha from the King and Queen," he said. "The Summer Solstice is tomorrow."

"What's that?" asked Wyatt.

"It's the first day of summer and the longest day of the year," explained Kimani. "The sun shines for the longest time tomorrow."

"Sasha, as the Lost Princess of the flying horses, it's time for your first assignment," said the toucan. "You are now in charge of the Summer Solstice celebration."

"Okay!" said Sasha. "I'll throw together a small party for the occasion."

"Oh, it's not going to be small. Not at all." The toucan shook his head.

"What do you mean?" asked Sasha.

"Per the King and Queen's orders, all the flying horses of Crystal Cove will gather in Verdant Valley to celebrate with the non-flying horses and come together as one," explained the toucan. "This party is a *very* big deal."

All the horses gathering in Verdant Valley? Sasha had been thinking something small with cake, decorations, and maybe a little singing, not an epic celebration!

"I have a to-do list for you." The toucan said, pulling a scroll of paper from under his wing. He unrolled it . . . and unrolled it . . . and unrolled it some more. The list went on and on and on!

"This looks pretty tricky," said her dad.

"Sasha is too young to throw such an important party," said her mom.

"No, I can handle this." Sasha didn't want her family to think she couldn't do it. She was the Lost Princess. A princess should be able to throw a big party. Sasha forced herself to stand taller. "I'm sure of it."

The next morning, Sasha and Kimani studied the long to-do list.

"What's the entertainment going to be?" asked Kimani.

"It's a dance." Sasha read out loud: "'The Maypole Dance is always performed during Summer Solstice celebrations. Four of the best dancers are needed: Two must be from Verdant Valley, and two dancers must be from Crystal Cove.'"

"I can be one dancer from Crystal Cove!" said Kimani.

"And I can be one dancer from Verdant Valley," said Sasha.

"We need two more," said Kimani.

"Who is the best dancer in Crystal Cove?" asked Sasha.

"My older brother, Malik, has amazing moves," Kimani said proudly.

Sasha had only visited the land of the flying horses a few times. She didn't know Malik. "Do you think he'd want to be a part of this?"

"I'll fly there and ask." With that, Kimani took to the sky.

Sasha stood in the shade of her family's cottonwood tree. She thought about possible dancers in Verdant Valley.

My mother can't dance.
My father won't dance.
Wyatt is too clumsy to dance.
Zara is too busy writing poetry to dance.

Sasha realized that left only her sister Poppy and her friend Twinkle. They were both great dancers.

Sasha trotted to the stream. Poppy and Twinkle were drinking the cool water. She told them she needed a great dancer for the celebration.

"All the flying horses from Crystal Cove will be coming to watch the Maypole Dance," she told them.

"Pick me," said Poppy. She did a shimmy and a shake.

"Pick me," said Twinkle. She did a whirl and a twirl.

Sasha looked at her sister. She looked at her friend. Who should she choose?

"I'm your sister," Poppy reminded her.

Sasha nodded. "You're right. I pick Poppy."

"What?" cried Twinkle. "I can stand on one hoof! I'm a much better dancer."

"It's just how the sister-thing works," explained Poppy.

Twinkle pouted. "That's not fair."

"I'll find something else for you to do," Sasha promised Twinkle.

"But—" started Twinkle.

"Sasha! Where are you?" Her father called her from far away.

Sasha hurried to the meadow.

Her father pointed to the tallest tree. "We can use this one for the maypole. I can string four long vines down from it."

"It's perfect," said Sasha. "The dancers will hold the vines in their teeth and dance around the tree."

She wanted to start practicing right away. She searched the sky. Kimani and her brother hadn't come back yet.

"What else can I do to help?" asked her dad.

"Can you make a stage?" asked Sasha.

"You got it." He was great at building things. Sasha asked Twinkle to help her dad. Twinkle agreed—but she didn't look all that happy.

Wyatt galloped over. "Give me a job, too!"

Sasha looked at the list. "This says that the four dancing horses must wear garlands made from the rare Citrus Cosmos flower."

"I've heard that flower smells like oranges and lemons," said Wyatt.

"Yum! Does it taste like oranges, too?" Sasha asked.

Wyatt shrugged. "I don't know. I've never tasted one."

"That must mean it's *really* rare. You've tasted every flower in Verdant Valley!" teased Sasha. Wyatt was always munching wildflowers. "Can you find it?"

"Maybe, but I don't know where to look," said Wyatt.

"Collie must know. She's a plant pixie, after all," said Sasha.

"Did someone say my name?" Collie said as she zoomed by. She didn't have wings, so she rode on the back of her hummingbird, Lucia. Lucia buzzed around the two horses.

"We're going on a flower hunt," said Sasha.

Collie clapped her tiny hands together in delight. The fairy knew where all the flowers grew. Even citrus ones.

Citrus Flowers

Sasha opened her wings.

Collie held on to Lucia, and Lucia opened her wings, too.

Wyatt stood on his huge magic flying leaf. Together, they flew to the top of Mystic Mountain.

"Under there!" Collie pointed to a crag on the side of the mountain. Velvety flowers bloomed underneath. Lucia fluttered close to the hidden flowers and the tiny fairy gathered them up. Then she sprinkled seeds and blew pixie breath on them to help them grow. Plant pixies never took flowers without planting new ones. They made sure the land stayed green and healthy.

Sasha placed the flowers carefully into a woven basket, and she, Wyatt, Collie, and Lucia brought them back to the meadow.

The smell of citrus filled the air. Wyatt licked his lips. "Please, just a small taste."

Sasha pulled the basket away. "My mother needs every flower to make the garlands."

"But they smell so good!" cried Wyatt.

Sasha wouldn't let Wyatt have a bite. One bite would lead to two . . . then three.

She quickly trotted over to her mother and gave her the basket.

Just then, Kimani touched down with another purple horse. "We're back!" she said and gestured to the other horse. "This is Malik."

Malik had a braided tail, just like Kimani. His coat was a deeper purple than Kimani's, and he stood two hands taller than his sister. His eyes flashed with flecks of silver, and he looked strong and confident.

Everyone hurried over to greet him. Then Sasha, Kimani, and Poppy gathered around the list the toucan had left behind. They studied the instructions for the dance.

"I don't need directions," said Malik. "I dance to the songs of the birds and the music of the wind."

He opened his wings wide. His long neck swayed and his tail twirled.

Sasha's mother stopped stringing garlands to watch. Her father stopped building the stage and stared in awe. Twinkle looked on with her mouth open in surprise. He was really good!

Malik liked being the center of attention. He high-stepped backward.

"You can't do it that way," said Sasha. "We need to do the dance as it's written. It's what the King and Queen want."

"That's silly." He huffed. "Okay, fine, whatever."

They got to work. The dance was tricky to learn. There were a lot of steps. Poppy always seemed to go the wrong way or do the wrong step.

"Poppy is ruining the dance," grumbled Malik.

"She just needs more practice," said Kimani.

"I can help," called Twinkle from where she was helping Sasha's dad with the stage.

"She's beyond help," quipped Malik.

"No, she's not." Sasha turned to Twinkle. "Don't worry, Twinkle. We've got this."

Malik showed Poppy the steps, but he danced too quickly. Poppy grew more and more confused by the routine.

"The garlands are done." Sasha's mother cantered over. She hung a necklace of flowers around Sasha's, Kimani's, Malik's, and Poppy's necks.

"The delicious smell makes me want to dance!" Malik performed the tricky steps.

"Me, too." Kimani joined in.

Poppy took a deep breath. She felt as if she were floating. Her hooves began to tap. Her legs began to prance.

"You're doing it!" cried Kimani.

"She is," agreed Malik. They all watched Poppy dance.

"The garland did it! I am never taking these flowers off!" cried Poppy.

chapter 4

Flower Power

With the garland of Citrus Cosmos flowers around her neck, Poppy was able to follow along with the routine, but the dance rehearsal wasn't going any more smoothly.

Malik pranced to the front. He blocked the others.

"Excuse me! This is a *group* dance," called Poppy.

"Yes, and I am the star of the group," said Malik.

"Says who?" demanded Poppy. The tips of her ears grew red with anger.

"Why don't we take a break?" Sasha suggested.

"Great idea," agreed Kimani. "Malik and Poppy could use some cooling off."

"Let's go to the Drinking Spot," said Poppy. "That's where the coolest water is."

"I'm not going with *you*," said Malik.

"Huh, whatever." Poppy rolled her eyes.

Sasha sighed as she, Poppy, and Kimani hung their garlands on the tree and trotted down to the stream. The celebration was supposed to be about horses getting along, but Malik and Poppy clearly didn't like each other.

"Where's Malik?" Kimani looked for her brother when they returned to the tree after their break.

Kimani reached for her garland. Sasha grabbed her own garland.

"Oh no!" cried Poppy.

Her necklace of flowers lay on the ground. Many of the petals had been torn or chewed off.

They all gasped. Who had done this?

At that moment, Malik flew down from behind a dark, puffy cloud.

"Where were you?!" demanded Poppy.

"Just stretching my wings. Why?"

Poppy held up her mangled garland. "Did *you* do this?"

Malik looked surprised. "What? It wasn't me. I was up in the sky the whole time."

"I won't be able to dance without my flowers now," cried Poppy.

"Maybe you don't need them," Kimani told Poppy. "Let's just try."

They took their positions around the maypole and each held a vine in their teeth.

"One . . . and two . . . and three . . . and dance," called Sasha.

Poppy froze. A horrified look crossed her face. "I can't remember the steps. I can't do the dance."

Sasha's stomach twisted. She needed to get Poppy a new garland. She called Collie for help.

"We picked all the citrus flowers already." Collie scratched her pointy chin. "But . . . I'll try to find some more."

"Please hurry," said Sasha. The celebration was only a few hours away.

"Kimani and I should do the dance by ourselves," offered Malik. "We'll make it two horses instead of four."

"That won't work," said Sasha. "The dance is for four horses. Besides, the point is to show flying and non-flying horses being together. Poppy is our only true non-flying horse. She *has* to be in the dance."

Malik sighed, annoyed.

"Sasha." Poppy pulled her sister to the side, whispering. "Malik is trying to kick me out of the dance. I think he destroyed my garland."

Rainbow Sprinkles

"Malik said he didn't do it," said Sasha.

"I don't believe him," said Poppy. "Do you?"

Sasha thought for a moment. She wasn't sure what to believe.

"Lunchtime!" Zara called. She and Twinkle appeared with a picnic basket.

Zara dished out carrot-apple pudding. Twinkle placed a tiny crab apple on the top of each one.

Malik took a bite. "Where's the zip? Where's the zing?"

"Zip? Zing?" Zara titled her head, not understanding.

"Food in Crystal Cove has magic in it," explained Kimani.

"I have something to make it magical." Malik held up a packet of rainbow sprinkles. He poured some sprinkles on top of everyone's pudding.

Sasha took a bite. "Wow! The pudding tastes amazing now!"

Both Zara and Twinkle agreed enthusiastically.

Poppy snorted. "I liked it just fine before."

"That can't be true." With a mischievous grin, Malik poured a heap of sprinkles on Poppy's pudding.

"Get off my food!" Poppy snatched her bowl away, scowling at Malik.

Just then, Collie flew in. Her pale green skin was smeared with dirt. Twigs poked out of her hair. Lucia held a small bundle of citrus flowers in her beak. "These are the very last ones until my seeds grow new flowers." Collie turned to Poppy. "Be very careful with them, okay?"

"Me? I didn't do anything." Poppy glared at Malik.

"We don't know what happened," Sasha reminded her.

Sasha brought the flowers to her mother to make a new garland. When she returned, Sasha found Poppy on the ground. Zara stood over her.

"What's wrong?" cried Sasha.

"I have a horrible bellyache," Poppy said with a groan.

"Do you think it was my pudding?" asked Zara.

"It couldn't be," said Sasha. "You make that pudding for us all the time. We've never gotten sick."

"We've never had it with magic sprinkles before," Poppy pointed out. "Malik gave me extra sprinkles on purpose. He knew they would make me sick."

"No way," said Malik. "I didn't do that."

Poppy groaned again, looking up at him. "My belly hurts too much to dance. You got what you wanted."

"I didn't want this!" insisted Malik.

"Yeah, right," said Poppy.

"That's not fair." Malik stomped off. Kimani hurried after him.

Zara helped Poppy back to their family's tree to rest.

"What are you going to do now?" Twinkle asked Sasha. "Everyone's gone. Who's going to dance?"

"I don't know," said Sasha.

"I could help," offered Twinkle.

"Thanks. I guess if Poppy doesn't feel better soon . . ." Sasha let her voice trail off as she walked across the meadow. There was so much to think about. Would Poppy feel better in time? Did Malik really do those terrible things?

Wyatt munched daisies near the stage. "Hey, what's wrong?" he asked when he saw tears pricking her eyes.

"The big Summer Solstice celebration is a big mess." Sasha filled him in on all that had happened.

"Did anyone see Malik ruin the garland or make Poppy sick?" asked Wyatt.

Sasha shook her head. "Right now, it's her word against his word."

"Hmm, you need proof," said Wyatt.

"If you think he did those things, you need to catch him in the act."

"Do you mean set a trap?" asked Sasha.

"Exactly," said Wyatt.

He leaned in to whisper in Sasha's ear. "Here's what you need to do."

Setting a Trap

"This NEW garland my mother made is more beautiful than the others!" Sasha spoke as loudly as she could a little while later. "It will make Poppy dance amazingly!"

All the horses were busy. Some cleared the grazing area. Others put up decorations. Twinkle worked on the stage. Malik and Kimani stretched their legs.

Dark rain clouds gathered overhead. Sasha raised her voice even louder. She needed to make sure everyone nearby heard her. "I am leaving the special GARLAND on top of this big ROCK. Poppy needs it to dance her best. But now, I must go FAR AWAY to find food for the celebration."

Then Sasha clopped away loudly.

Except she didn't go far. She tucked herself behind a row of bushes. It was the perfect hiding place. She could see the garland on the big rock, but no one could see her.

Her plan was simple. She would wait until Malik came. If he tried to destroy Poppy's new garland, she'd catch him in the act.

Sasha waited and waited.

No one came near the rock.

The sky grew darker as rain began to fall. The horses left the meadow to find shelter under trees.

Sasha didn't like standing by herself. It was getting dark—and spooky.

Suddenly, she heard a rustle behind her. Then footsteps in the tall grass. Sasha gulped.

Who else was out here?

She squinted through the rain. She couldn't see anything.

The footsteps grew closer.

Sasha held her breath.

A dark figure stepped toward her. "I brought you a blanket."

Sasha knew that voice. "Dad? Is that you?"

It was! Her dad wrapped her in a blanket made from ferns. "I came to keep you company. I heard you and Wyatt talking. I know all about your plan."

Sasha smiled at the warmth of the blanket and of having her dad nearby. She gave him a nuzzle. "Thanks."

For a long time, they stood in silence. The rain slowed to a drizzle.

Maybe Poppy had been wrong. Sasha was about to give up when her dad whispered, "Wait! Look there!"

CHAPTER 7) The Chase

A horse approached the big rock—and reached for the garland.

Was it Malik? In the gray mist, Sasha couldn't quite see the thief's face.

The horse snatched the garland and put it around its neck. It began to trot away.

"Stop!" cried Sasha.

The thief didn't stop. Its trot turned into a canter.

Sasha sprang out from behind the bushes. She galloped toward the figure Her dad ran alongside her.

The horse heard their pounding hooves and increased to a full-speed gallop, too.

Sasha kept her eyes fixed on the horse's tail. She needed to get closer. She willed herself to run faster . . . faster. . . .

Sasha and her dad ran side by side. Across the meadow. Over a hill. Around a tree. Her dad couldn't dance, but he could sure run fast.

Up ahead, the crook reached the stream. The only way across was through the cold water. The thief splashed down into the water.

Sasha had another way across. She opened her wings. She shook out her sparkly feathers and rose into the sky. Sasha landed on the other side of the stream—right in front of the thief!

The horse whirled around to see Sasha's dad now standing right behind him.

With Sasha in front and Sasha's dad behind, the criminal was trapped.

"Who are you? Show yourself!" Sasha demanded.

The thief lifted its head.

The Show Must Go On

"Twinkle?!" Sasha cried.

She had never expected the thief to be a friend of hers. It wasn't Malik after all.

"Twinkle, why did you take Poppy's garland?" Sasha asked.

Twinkle climbed out of the stream. "Because I wanted to dance. I know she's your sister, Sasha, but you said you wanted the *best* dancer. That's me."

"So you tried to keep Poppy from dancing?" asked Sasha.

Twinkle nodded. "She needed the garland to dance, so I tore the petals off. And I put a rotten crabapple on her pudding to give her a bellyache. I thought if she couldn't dance, you'd have to pick me instead."

"That's horrible! You could've made her really sick," cried Sasha.

"I'm so sorry. I guess I got too carried away." Twinkle flattened her ears.

Sasha could see how bad she felt.

"Hey, Sasha, they're all here." Her dad stretched his neck to gesture toward the sky. Red, blue, purple, green, and pink horses flew in for the celebration, with the toucan leading the charge. "The sun is coming out, too."

"You can give Poppy her garland." Twinkle lowered her head so Sasha could remove the garland from around her neck.

Sasha, her dad, and Twinkle hurried back to the meadow. Sasha still had a big party to throw.

They gathered around the cottonwood tree with Sasha's family, Wyatt, Malik, and Kimani. Twinkle apologized to Poppy. Sasha and Poppy apologized to Malik for suspecting him.

"Are you ready to do the dance?" asked Sasha.

"I can't." Poppy groaned. "My belly still hurts too much."

"I'm ready," said Malik.

"Me, too," said Kimani.

"That's only three dancers," Sasha said. There are four vines hanging from the maypole. The directions say that we need *four* horses." She stared at the horses from Crystal Cove and Verdant Valley gathered around the stage. And now she didn't have enough dancers.

Now her stomach hurt, too!

"This was my first assignment as a princess, and now it's all messed up." Sasha took a step toward the waiting audience. "I guess I'll tell them there won't be a dance."

"Wait! I can dance with you," said her dad. "I saw you practicing while I was building the stage."

"But you hate to dance," said Sasha.

"I love you more than I hate to dance," he said.

"Um, I may be clumsy, but I'll dance with you." Wyatt stepped forward.

"And I don't know the steps, but I can try, too," added Zara.

Everyone wanted to help Sasha.

CHAPTER 9) Just Dance

Suddenly, Sasha had plenty of dancers. They weren't great dancers like the directions said.

So what? Does that even matter? Sasha wondered.

She knew the answer. She whispered into her father's ear, and he hurried away.

"Who's going to be the fourth dancer?" asked Wyatt. "Is it me?"

Sasha gave him a secret smile. She stepped onto the stage.

"Welcome to the Summer Solstice celebration!" she called out as the gathered horses quieted down. "The sun is shining as we celebrate the longest day of the year with flying and non-flying horses together as one."

The horses cheered, neighed, and brayed.

"We are now all equally friends. That means there is no star, and no one is left out. It also means that not only the four best dancers get to dance." She turned and smiled at the maypole. Dozens of vines now hung down from it. Her dad had quickly strung them all up. "Everyone grab a vine and dance with us!"

"What about the steps and the directions?" asked Malik.

"Forget the directions. Just dance to the songs of the birds and the music of the wind." Sasha grinned at him.

"Awesome!" Malik began to groove.

The toucan led the birds in the nearby trees in song.

All the flying and non-flying horses grabbed vines. They twirled around the maypole. Some horses flew. Others couldn't. Wyatt tripped and knocked into Zara, and Sasha's dad got tangled up. The dance was a royal mess, but no one seemed to mind as they all laughed.

Everyone was having much more fun now as they danced together.

Sasha's mom took apart the garlands. She went around and tucked one citrus flower into each dancer's mane.

"I'm feeling better," called Poppy.

Malik helped her up. He gave her a vine.

Twinkle came over to Sasha. "I'm so glad Poppy is okay. I was wrong to try to stop her from being able to perform so I could get what I wanted. I know that now."

Sasha reached for the last free vine. She passed it to Twinkle.

"For me? . . . But why?" asked Twinkle.

"Everyone deserves to dance," said Sasha.

Twinkle's eyes twinkled as she joined in the fun.

The toucan landed on Sasha's back. "Princess, you've done a great job."

"Thanks!" Sasha grinned.

"Your work as a royal is just beginning," he told her. "But you're off to a marvelous start!"

"Thank you!" said Sasha and danced the day away with all the horses.

Read on for a sneak peek
from the ninth book in the
Tales of Sasha series!

Tales of
SASHA
The Disappearing History

by Alexa Pearl

illustrated by Paco Sordo

CHAPTER 1

A Royal Horse

"Come out, come out, wherever you fly!" called Kimani.

Sasha ducked behind a cloud. It was big and heavy with raindrops. She flapped her wings, hovering in place. She stayed very quiet.

Does Kimani see me? wondered Sasha.

No! Her friend Kimani flew right by.

Sasha still didn't move. The twins, Marigold and Sonali, were playing hide-and-seek, too. Sasha searched the sky. She didn't see them anywhere.

Suddenly, Marigold zoomed up behind her. She reached out her hoof and tagged Sasha. "I found you!"

"Where did you come from?" cried

Sasha.

Marigold pointed to another cloud below. "There's a horse behind every cloud!"

Playing hide-and-seek with flying horses on a cloudy day was tricky!

"My turn to hide." Marigold's bright-yellow body streaked away across the sky.

Kimani darted after Marigold to look for a hiding spot as well. Her violet feathers flapped fast.

Sasha took off, too. The wind rushed across her face and ruffled her white mane. She loved flying at top speed.

"Whoa!" cried Sasha as the Toucan suddenly flew in front of her.

"Toodle-loo! Sapphire wants to see you!" he called.

"Right after I find Marigold." Sasha didn't want to stop playing the game.

"Oh, no, no, no," said the Toucan. "Sapphire means right now."

Sapphire was in charge of the flying horses that lived in Crystal Cove and the Toucan was her messenger. So everyone did what Sapphire asked—including Sasha.

Sasha followed the Toucan down to the Crystal Cove beach. The sand sparkled with jewels and gems. The flying horses lived inside caves carved into the rocky cliff. But instead of leading Sasha to the golden door of Sapphire's home, the Toucan brought her to a red door.

"Where are we?" Sasha had never been inside this cave.

"The Royal Library," said the Toucan.

"Important books and maps are kept here." He tapped the door five times with the tip of his beak.

Sapphire opened the door. "Welcome, Princess!" Sapphire's wing feathers shined deep blue. Sapphire was one of the oldest horses in Crystal Cove.

"Oh, please, Sapphire. You should call me Sasha." Sasha rocked back on her hooves. "Princess sounds so . . . serious."

"Being the Lost Princess is serious," said Sapphire. "Important, too."

"Yes, I know." It felt so strange to be the Lost Princess of the flying horses. Up until a little while ago, Sasha hadn't known she was a flying horse. Sometimes she still couldn't believe that she could fly.

Sasha stepped into the Royal Library and gasped. "It's so beautiful."

Shelves reached from the floor to the ceiling as far as she could see. They were filled with hundreds of books in all the colors of the rainbow and ancient-looking, rolled-up scrolls. Huge maps decorated the ceiling. Sasha stared in wonder.

"I've called you here for this." Sapphire led her to a golden table in the middle of the library. A thick scroll lay on it. "This contains the history of the flying horses." She unrolled the scroll. It was made of enchanted fabric. The long tapestry spilled over the side of the table and across the floor. "It's time for you to read these old stories. As a royal horse, they must become part of you."

Shelves reached almost the door to the ceilings as to as the counter top. They were filled with ... of bottles in ... precision of the ... and under ... looking, roll-up small ... little pear decorated with ... filling Stash ... line in ...

... we rolled gen... here ... this ... sapphire led him to a bottle visible in the middle of the ... A ... lettered inscription ... "This contains the history of the ... horses." And under it ... ... that it was made of ... used table. The ... reading ... over the sofa. ... of the table one as ... the floor. Its ... to reach these ... letters. As a small bottle, it ... over scent pert... about ...